OCT 0 9 2015

Freddie Fernortner

FEARLESS FIRST GRADER ©

Freddie   Darla   Chipper   Mr. Chewy

THE SUPER-SCARY NIGHT THINGY

BY JOHNATHAN RAND

D0033287

OCT 8 9 2015

An AudioCraft Publishing, Inc. book

This book is a work of fiction. Names, places, characters and incidents are used fictitiously, or are products of the author's very active imagination.

No part of this publication may be reproduced in whole or in part, or stored in a retrieval system, or transmitted in any form or by any means, electronic, mechanic, photocopying, recording, or otherwise, without written permission from the publisher. For information regarding permission, write to: AudioCraft Publishing, Inc., PO Box 281, Topinabee Island, MI 49791

Freddie Fernortner, Fearless First Grader Book 2:
The Super-Scary Night-Thingy
ISBN 13-digit: 978-1-893699-80-9

Librarians/Media Specialists:
PCIP/MARC records available **free of charge** at
www.americanchillers.com

Cover and interior illustrations by
Cartoon Studios, Battle Creek, MI
Cover layout and design by Sue Harring

Copyright © 2005 AudioCraft Publishing, Inc. All rights reserved.
AMERICAN CHILLERS® , MICHIGAN CHILLERS® and
FREDDIE FERNORTNER, FEARLESS FIRST GRADER® are
registered trademarks of
AudioCraft Publishing, Inc.

Dickinson Press Inc., Grand Rapids MI, USA • Job 3778300 September 2010

THE
SUPER-SCARY
NIGHT THINGY

VISIT CHILLERMANIA!

WORLD HEADQUARTERS FOR BOOKS BY JOHNATHAN RAND!

Yooperland

Indian River

Alpena

Traverse City

MICHIGAN

Mt. Pleasant

Bay City

Grand Rapids

Lansing

Detroit

Kalamazoo

CHILLERMANIA!

**I-75 Exit 313
then south
1 mile!**

Visit the HOME for books by Johnathan Rand! Featuring books, hats, shirts, bookmarks and other cool stuff not available anywhere else in the world! Plus, watch the American Chillers website for news of special events and signings at *CHILLERMANIA!* with author Johnathan Rand! Located in northern lower Michigan, on I-75! Take exit 313 . . . then south 1 mile! For more info, call (231) 238-0338. And be afraid! Be veeeery afraaaaaaiiiid . . . .

1

"Help me get this tent into the back yard," Freddie Fernortner said to his two friends, Darla and Chipper. The three first graders were in Freddie's garage, where they had just found the Fernortner's small tent. Sometimes, Freddie and his family used it when they went camping.

Tonight, however, the three children were going to use the tent for a different reason.

They were going to set up the tent in

Freddie's back yard.

Then, they would wait until it got dark.

Until the shadows grew long.

Until the crickets started chirping, and bats flitted through the sky.

Until the big silvery moon gazed down upon them.

Then, they were going to go into the tent and read scary stories from a book that Freddie had checked out from the local library.

In the dark, with only a flashlight.

"Gosh, this thing is heavy," Chipper said as he helped Freddie with the tent. Darla was carrying the long, wooden stakes. Mr. Chewy, Freddie's cat, was sitting near the garage door, chewing on a wad of gum and blowing bubbles. He was the only cat in the world who could do that, and

Freddie was quite proud of himself for teaching the animal how to do it.

And that's how the cat got its name.

Mr. Chewy.

The three kids carried the tent and the stakes into the back yard.

"We need to set it up in a place that will be spooky," Freddie said.

"How can a back yard be spooky?" Darla said, looking around. "There's nothing scary here."

For sure, Freddie's back yard looked a lot like any other back yard. There were several trees, a cement birdbath, and a small inflatable wading pool that Freddie sometimes used during the hot summer days. Near the fence was a picnic table and a barbeque grill, where Freddie's dad often grilled hamburgers and hot dogs on the weekends.

But there wasn't anything that was scary.

"Let's set it up under that tree over there," Chipper said.

"Good idea," Freddie agreed. "It might be even darker under the tree, because the leaves will block out the moon."

It didn't take long to set up the tent. Freddie had helped his father with it many times, and he knew exactly how to put it together. It was dark green and was held up by two wooden stakes and a few small ropes that were fastened to smaller stakes that were pushed into the ground.

"There," Freddie said as the last stake was set. "Now we're ready."

"Now what?" Darla said.

"Let's meet here just before dark," Freddie said. "I'll get our flashlight that Mom keeps in the kitchen drawer. And I'll bring the scary book that I checked out from the library."

"This is going to be spooky!" Chipper said.

"I can't wait!" said Darla.

"It's going to be fun, that's for sure,"

Freddie said.

But Freddie, Darla, and Chipper had no idea just how scary the night would turn out to be.

2

The sun went down.

The moon came up.

Bats whirled through the night sky.

Crickets chirped.

And Freddie, Darla, Chipper, and Mr. Chewy were huddled together in the small tent. The only light came from the beam of the flashlight Freddie held in his hand.

"This is so cool!" Darla whispered.

"Yeah," Chipper said. "I like to read

stories in bed, under the covers, with a flashlight. But being out in a tent is going to be a lot more fun!"

Somewhere in the distance, an owl hooted.

"I'll bet it's a great horned owl," Chipper said. "My dad saw it a few nights ago. He said it was huge!"

"I'd like to see that sometime," Freddie said.

"Dad says that you don't see them very often," Chipper continued, "because they only come out at night."

Freddie picked up his library book. "What story should we read first?" he asked.

"A good one," Chipper said.

"A scary one," Darla said. "One that will give me the shivers."

"There are lots of good ones in the

book," Freddie said. "Stories about ghosts and haunted houses and werewolves."

"Just don't read any stories about super-scary night thingys," Darla warned. Her eyes grew wide. "That would be *too* scary."

Chipper frowned. "Super-scary night thingys?" he asked. "What are super-scary night thingys?"

"Yeah," Freddie said. "What are super-scary night thingys?"

"Super-scary night thingys are just terrible," Darla said. Her eyes grew wide. "My older brother told me all about them. He's in fourth grade, so he's really smart. He says that super-scary night thingys can be anywhere . . . in a closet, under the bed, outside in the bushes, anywhere."

"But what are they?" Freddie prodded.

"Super-scary night thingys are weird creatures that can disappear and appear whenever they want to," Darla said. "Some of them are very big, and some of them are very small. But they're very scary."

"What do they look like?" Chipper asked.

Darla shrugged. "I don't really know," she said. "My brother says that they are so scary looking that he couldn't even talk about it."

"There is no such thing as super-scary night thingys," Freddie said. "Your brother was just trying to scare you because you're in first grade, and he's in fourth."

"No, they're real," Darla insisted. "I heard one once. Under my bed."

"Did you see it?" Chipper asked.

"When I looked, it was already gone. They can disappear whenever they want, you know."

Outside, a gentle breeze rustled the tree branches above. The moon shone down, brightening the sides of the tent.

"Well, I say we start reading right at the beginning of the book," Freddie said. "That way, we won't miss anything."

"You start," said Chipper.

"Yeah," Darla agreed. "Start reading, Freddie."

"Okay," Freddie said. "Here goes."

But Freddie didn't even get a chance to read.

Because right at that moment, there was a noise from outside.

The three first graders turned—and saw the shadow of a huge monster on the tent!

3

All three children shrieked.

They huddled close.

Freddie pointed the flashlight at the tent flap.

The tent flap began to open.

The three screamed again.

The monster tossed back the flap and said:

"What's going on out here?"

Freddie, Darla, and Chipper breathed

sighs of relief. It wasn't a monster, after all! It was Freddie's mom!

"I brought you some popcorn," she said. "I didn't mean to scare you."

"I love popcorn!" Darla said.

"Yeah!" Chipper said. "Thanks, Mrs. Fernortner!"

Mrs. Fernortner knelt down and handed Freddie a big bowl filled with hot, buttery popcorn. Then she handed each child a napkin.

"Have fun," she said. "And don't scare yourselves silly."

"We won't, Mom," Freddie said.

"She's a cool mom," Chipper said, after Mrs. Fernortner had left.

"Yeah, I think I'm going to keep her around," Freddie said. "Sometimes, she even lets me eat cookies in bed while I read."

"I wish my mom let me do that," Darla said, crossing her arms.

Freddie placed the bowl of popcorn in the middle, and the three kids ate hungrily.

"Okay," Freddie said, still munching on a mouthful of popcorn. "Let's get started. Here we go."

And Freddie read.

The story was good.

It was creepy.

It was scary.

But it was a story . . . and that's why Freddie, Darla, and Chipper didn't get scared.

But they were about to.

Because something scary was about to happen . . . for real.

4

Freddie had just finished reading a page. Mr. Chewy was next to him, laying down. He had gone to sleep.

Again, they heard the owl hoot in the distance. Freddie again hoped that he would see it someday.

"Okay," he said. "Chipper, it's your turn to read."

He handed Chipper the scary book.

"This is a lot of fun!" Chipper said.

"We should do this again tomorrow night!"

"Every night!" Darla exclaimed.

Chipper picked up where Freddie left off. The story was a good one . . . about a ghost that lived in the basement of an old home. It wasn't a *true* story, but it was a *good* story.

After Chipper had read a few pages, he handed the book to Darla. Darla was a very good reader, and while she read, she glanced up at Freddie and Chipper and made spooky faces.

Suddenly, Darla was interrupted by a terrible sound outside. It sounded like a deep, scratchy growl—but scarier.

All three first graders jumped.

Darla stopped reading.

They huddled close.

"What . . . what was . . . that?" Chipper stammered quietly.

"I . . . I don't know," Freddie replied. "I've never heard it before."

"It's a super-scary night thingy!" Darla said. "I know it is! That's what they sound like!"

"There's no such thing as super-scary night thingys," Chipper hissed.

"Yes, there is," Darla said. "And that's what they sound like."

"It's probably just the wind," Freddie said. "Come on. Let's go find out."

He scooted toward the front of the tent.

"Are you crazy?!?!" Darla said. "Super-scary night thingys can swallow first graders in one gulp!"

"Who told you that?" Freddie asked. Mr. Chewy was awake now, looking around the tent at the three first graders.

"My older brother told me," Darla

whispered.

"*Well, if all three of us go and look, the super-scary night thingy can't get us,*" Freddie said.

"*Says who?*" Darla said.

"*Says me,*" Freddie said. "*Come on. Let's go find out.*"

"*Freddie's right,*" Chipper whispered. "*It's probably just the wind.*"

Chipper scooted to where Freddie was at the front of the tent.

"*I'll go with you,*" Darla said. "*But just for the record: I don't think this is a good idea at all.*"

"*Here,*" Freddie said, holding out the flashlight for Chipper. "*Hold this.*"

Chipper took the flashlight.

Freddie unzipped the tent flap.

Their scary adventure was about to begin.

5

The three children knelt at the front of the tent, staring out into the darkness. Lights from other homes glowed yellow and white through windows.

But Freddie's back yard was dark.

It was spooky.

Chipper handed the flashlight back to Freddie. Freddie swept the beam around.

Nothing.

"Where did the sound come from?"

Chipper asked.

"Over there, I think," Freddie said, pointing with the flashlight. "Near the back fence."

"It sure is dark over there," Darla said.

"Yeah," Freddie agreed, "but we have a flashlight. Come on."

Freddie crawled out of the tent. Chipper and Darla followed. Mr. Chewy stayed in the tent, chewing on a wad of gum.

"Let's go real slow," Freddie said.

The three first graders huddled together as they moved very slowly across the lawn.

Suddenly, a shape came into view. The three stopped.

"What's that?" Chipper asked.

"It's only the birdbath," Freddie said.

And that's all it was. They continued walking. As they drew nearer, they could see the birdbath clearer. But, as they drew even closer, Darla gasped.

She pointed at something in the beam of the flashlight.

Something in the birdbath.

Then she froze.

"Look!" she suddenly shrieked. "It's horrible! Oh, my! It's *terrible!*"

Chipper and Freddie looked at what she was pointing at.

Chipper gasped.

Even Freddie gasped. "I can't believe it!" he exclaimed.

There was no water in the birdbath, but there was something else . . . *and that something was a full set of human teeth!*

6

Freddie stared into the birdbath.

He trained the flashlight on the set of teeth in the large bowl.

"I can't believe we found them," he said.

Darla and Chipper were horrified.

"Are they . . . are they real?" Darla asked.

"Well, not really *real*," Freddie replied. "They're false. And they happen to belong to my grandpa."

"Your grandpa lost his teeth?!?!" Chipper exclaimed.

"Last weekend we had a cookout," Freddie explained. "My dad told a joke, and my grandpa laughed so hard that he accidentally spit out his false teeth. We looked all over the yard, but we didn't find them. And no wonder! We never looked in the birdbath! Boy, my grandpa is going to be happy about this."

"What are we going to do with them?" Darla asked.

"I'm not touching them," Freddie said. "They've been in my grandpa's mouth."

"I'm not touching them, either," Chipper said.

"Count me out," Darla said.

"We'll leave them here," Freddie said.

"I'll tell mom. Let *her* come out here and pick them up."

"She'll probably wear gloves," Darla said. "I would, if I had to pick up someone's false teeth."

And that's when it happened.

They heard the noise again.

Louder. Closer.

Freddie, Darla, and Chipper jumped.

They spun around.

The sound had come from behind the bushes near the garage.

"It's over there somewhere," Freddie said, real quiet-like. "Let's go."

The three clung to each other. Freddie held the flashlight out like a sword as they approached the garage.

Closer.

Tiptoeing.

Closer.

They stopped, just before they reached the bushes.

And it was then that the super-scary night thingy attacked.

7

The creature came at them so quickly that there was no time for the three first graders to even move.

They couldn't run.

They couldn't scream.

They could only gasp—

As the scared rabbit came out of its hiding place and hopped quickly away.

Yes, that's all it was. A bunny rabbit, hiding behind the bushes. Actually,

Freddie, Darla, and Chipper probably scared the small animal worse than it had scared them.

"Oh my gosh!" Darla finally said. She heaved a heavy sigh of relief. "I thought I was going to faint!"

"Some super-scary night thingy that turned out to be," Chipper smirked.

"But where did that other noise come from?" Freddie asked. "We all heard it. I don't think a rabbit could have made a noise like that."

Freddie swept the beam over the yard. They could just barely make out the picnic table near the fence. The barbeque grill stood next to it like a shadowy ghost.

"Well, whatever it was," Chipper said, "I think it's gone now."

"Of course," Darla said. "That's what super-scary night thingys do. They can appear and disappear whenever they want to. That's why they're so scary. Why, there might be one watching us at this very moment."

The three were silent for a few seconds. Just thinking that, at that very moment, a super-scary night thingy might be nearby gave all three of them chills.

"Well, whatever it was, it's gone," Freddie said. "Come on. Let's go back to the tent and keep reading. We were just getting to a really scary part."

"Besides," Chipper said. "We're letting the popcorn get cold."

The three first graders, still knotted together, walked across the lawn. The grass was cold and damp with dew.

Crickets chimed.

Bats flew overhead.

Lights in other houses glowed, but

Freddie's back yard was dark and gloomy.

There is no such thing as super-scary night thingys, Freddie thought. *Darla's brother was just making that up to scare her.*

Wasn't he?

Freddie wasn't so sure.

And it was at that very moment that two glowing eyes appeared in the darkness.

8

Freddie, Darla, and Chipper froze.

Ahead of them, not more than ten feet away, were two glowing, yellow eyes.

"It's a super-scary night thingy!" Darla hissed. Her voice was filled with fear.

Freddie and Chipper didn't respond. They weren't sure what the eyes belonged to. Maybe it really *was* a super-scary night thingy.

Or maybe something *worse*.

Freddie shined the flashlight toward the eyes, but it wasn't bright enough to show the creature.

And while they were standing there, huddled in the darkness, a strange thing happened.

One of the yellow eyes began to move.

It drifted upward, moving back and forth, until Freddie suddenly realized what they were seeing.

"That's not a super-scary night thingy!" he cried. "Those are just two fireflies!"

Sure enough, when they walked closer, they could see the remaining firefly sitting on the fence. It glowed bright yellow, and when the trio got too close, it flew away, spinning up into the night sky, where it vanished.

"Whew," Chipper said. "That really freaked me out. For a minute, I thought they were the eyes of a monster."

"Yeah, that was kind of scary," Freddie said with a chuckle. "I'm glad it wasn't a monster."

Not far away, lights glowed in Freddie's house. Freddie could see the shadow of his mother through the kitchen window.

"Let's go back inside the tent," he said. "I'll have to go inside and get ready for bed in a little while, but we still have time to read more from my scary book."

Freddie used the flashlight to light their way, and the three friends walked across the dark lawn.

They reached the tent, and Chipper pulled back the flap. Mr. Chewy sat inside, still chewing on a wad of gum.

But just as Freddie knelt down to crawl into the tent, they heard the noise again.

And this time, it was closer.

Louder.

And it was a scraping sound.

Like . . . .

Claws.

Freddie shuddered.

Darla shook.

Chipper trembled.

And the sound came again.

Freddie turned and shined the light around. When the three first graders saw what was making the noise, they shrieked in terror.

On the other side of the fence was the dark shadow of a super-scary night thingy!

9

"*See?*" Darla whispered. Her voice trembled. "*I told you they were real!*"

Freddie moved the light back and forth. The monster was on the other side of the fence, and all they could see was its shadowy form.

Its claw scraped the fence again, making the three first graders to jump. Even Mr. Chewy flinched and stopped chewing his gum.

"Wait a minute," Freddie said. Bravely, he took a step closer to the fence.

"Freddie!" Chipper hissed. "What are you doing?!?! That thing is going to eat you up!"

Freddie didn't say anything. Instead, he took yet another step forward.

"That's not a monster!" he suddenly cried. "It's a bush!"

He walked quickly over to the fence and shined the light on the other side.

"See?" he said. "It's just a bush. The wind is causing a branch to scrape against the fence."

"I knew that," Chipper said. "I was just waiting for you to figure it out."

"You were not," Darla said. "You thought that it was a super-scary night thingy."

"Did not!"

"Did too!"

Freddie walked back to the tent. He knelt down, pushed open the flap, and scrambled inside. Darla and Chipper followed. The three sat in a circle around the popcorn bowl. Each clawed a handful of popcorn and began munching.

"Chipper's turn to read," Freddie said, and he handed him the scary book.

And Chipper started to read.

Freddie and Darla listened.

They ate popcorn.

Mr. Chewy chewed gum.

None of them were aware, however, that when they had left the tent, something had gotten inside.

Something they couldn't see.

Something that was only seconds away from attacking.

10

The popcorn bowl was almost empty, and Chipper was almost finished reading when it happened. He was at a very, very scary part in the book. It was so scary that Darla and Freddie held hands.

Suddenly, the bloodthirsty creature attacked . . . and it bit Chipper's neck!

"Aaaah!" Chipper cried, so loudly that Freddie and Darla nearly jumped out of their skins!

Chipper dropped the book, knocking over the popcorn bowl. Both of his hands when to his neck.

"Ouch!" he cried. "That hurt!"

"What?!?!" Freddie asked. "What was it?!?!"

"A mosquito!" Chipper said. "It bit me on the neck!"

Freddie shined the light on Chipper's neck. Sure enough, there was a small droplet of blood where the insect had bitten him.

"I think you'll live," Freddie said. He shined the light around the tent, until he found a large mosquito on the tent flap. Freddie swatted at it and missed. Instead, the insect flew outside through the small crack between the two flaps.

"Next time let's bring the bug spray," Chipper said, rubbing his neck. "Why, that thing could have sucked a gallon of blood out of me!"

"Make sure there aren't any more," Darla said. "I don't want any of those things biting me. I'm only a little girl, and I don't have a lot of blood to lose, you know."

Freddie swept the flashlight beam around the tent. When he was sure that there were no more mosquitos, he picked up the scary book.

"My turn," he said, opening the book. "I'll find another good story."

He flipped through the pages until he found another ghost story.

"Hey, this one sounds cool," he said. "It's about a ghost that haunts an old schoolhouse in a small town called Great Bear Heart. It says here that it's a true story."

"Ghost stories aren't true," Freddie said. "They're just made-up. Like super-scary night thingys."

Darla glared at him. "You're just afraid to admit that they're real," she said.

"Am not," Chipper shot back. "There's no such thing."

"Is too."

"Is not! And I'll prove it!"

"How?" Darla asked.

"Yeah," Freddie said. "How are you going to prove it?"

"Well," Chipper began, "we've been sitting here in this tent reading scary stories. But the scariest things that have happened to us haven't been in the book. Plus, the things that scared us weren't even scary. Think about it: we've been scared by false teeth, a rabbit, two fireflies, a bush, and a mosquito."

"Yeah?" Darla said. "So?"

"So, those aren't things we should be afraid of. As a matter of fact, there is nothing in the yard to be afraid of. Not even super-scary night thingys."

"You'll change your mind when you see one," Darla warned.

Chipper rolled onto his knees.

He crawled toward the tent flap.

He pushed the tent flap open.

"I'll prove that there isn't anything in the yard to be afraid of," he said. "I'll go walk around without the flashlight."

And with that, he ducked out of the tent and vanished.

"Oooh, he shouldn't do that," Darla said nervously.

"He'll be okay," Freddie said.

They waited.

And listened.

Chipper's voice called out to them. He was far away, on the other side of the yard.

"See?" he shouted, his voice echoing through the neighborhood. "There's nothing out here. Nothing to be afraid of at all. I don't think—"

His voice was suddenly cut off.

And he started screaming.

11

When Freddie and Darla heard Chipper
scream, they knew he wasn't fooling
around. Chipper's shrieks were too real,
too *scary,* and they knew that their friend
was in deep trouble.

"Chipper!" Freddie shouted, and he
scrambled out of the tent. Darla followed.

"See?!?!" she said. "I told you they
were real! I told you that super-scary night

thingys are real!"

Chipper had stopped screaming, but Freddie and Darla could hear the sounds of a struggle. Chipper grunted and groaned.

"We've got to save him!" Freddie said.

"Shouldn't we go get your mom and dad?" Darla asked.

"There isn't any time!" Freddie said. "Chipper! Chipper! Can you hear me?!?!"

Chipper was silent, and Freddie started walking across the dark yard, waving the flashlight beam back and forth. "Chipper?!?!"

"I'm over here," Chipper gasped.

"Where?!?!" Freddie asked. "Keep talking so I can find you."

"Right here," Chipper said.

Suddenly, Chipper's form came into view. He was on the ground, struggling to get up.

"What happened?" Darla asked. "Was it a super-scary night thingy?"

"Worse," Chipper replied.

"What can be worse than a super-scary night thingy?" Darla said.

"A wading pool," Chipper replied sheepishly. "I was walking along, and I didn't see it in the dark. I fell in."

When they got closer, Freddie and Darla could see that he was soaked from head to toe. His hair was wet, and it stuck to his head. His clothing dripped.

"I have to go home and get dried off," he said. He stood up. "Besides . . . it's getting late. I'm going to have to go to bed soon."

"Yeah, me too," Darla said. "I'm sure glad you didn't get eaten by a super-scary night thingy."

Chipper didn't say anything.

"I'll walk you home with the flashlight," Freddie offered. "You, too, Darla."

The three first graders began walking. Mr. Chewy followed.

"Tonight was a lot of fun," Freddie said.

"Yeah," Darla agreed. "And that was

nice of your mom to make popcorn."

"I had fun, too," Chipper said, "even though I fell into your wading pool."

They walked across the street to Chipper's house. The front porch light was burning brightly. Chipper took off his wet shoes and socks and left them by the door. Mr. Chewy sniffed Chipper's socks.

"My mom is going to freak when she sees me all soaked like this," Chipper said.

"Sorry about that," said Freddie.

"Hey, it wasn't your fault," Chipper replied.

He grasped the knob and opened the door.

"See you guys tomorrow," he said.

"See you later," Freddie said.

"Good night," Darla said.

Chipper stepped inside and closed the door.

Freddie and Darla stepped off the porch and headed back across the street. Mr. Chewy scampered after them.

"Darla," Freddie began, "do you think that your brother was just trying to fool you? You know . . . about the super-scary night thingys?"

"I'm not sure," Darla replied. "I mean . . . I've never seen one. But my brother says you never know where they might be."

Several lights glowed from within Darla's house. They walked to the front porch.

"Tell your mom thanks for the popcorn," Darla said.

"I will," Freddie promised. "See you in the morning."

"Okay," Darla said, and she opened the door and vanished inside.

Freddie turned and looked around the neighborhood. Streetlights shined, and lights in houses glowed. Above, the moon shimmered. Stars twinkled.

And he thought about super-scary night thingys.

They aren't real, he thought. *Darla's brother just made that up to scare her.*

Just when he and Mr. Chewy reached the front porch of his own house, Freddie stopped.

My book, he thought. *I left my scary book in the tent.*

"Stay here," he said to Mr. Chewy. The cat, still chewing a wad of gum, sat obediently on the first step.

Freddie stepped off the porch and walked around to the side of the house.

He walked into the dark back yard.

Toward the tent.

Of course, he had no idea that something was in the tent, waiting for him.

Not a mosquito.

Not a rabbit.

Not a firefly.

Not his scary book.

Something that was *much* bigger.

And when he saw the huge, dark shape coming out of the tent, Freddie knew that he was in a lot of trouble.

12

At that moment, Freddie was so frightened that he dropped the flashlight. He wished that Chipper and Darla were with him.

He wished that Mr. Chewy was with him.

He wished that he didn't have to face the super-scary night thingy alone.

The giant figure moved toward him.

"Please, Mr. Super-Scary Night Thingy," Freddie begged. "Please don't hurt me."

"Who are you talking to?" a voice asked.

Instantly, Freddie was relieved, because he recognized the voice of his father.

"Whew," Freddie gasped. "It's only you. I thought it was a super-scary night thingy."

"A what?" his father asked.

"Never mind," Freddie said.

"Your mother asked me to come out and get you. It's time to get ready for bed."

"Okay," said Freddie. "I just have to get my book out of the tent."

Freddie picked up the flashlight and strode to the tent. His scary book and the popcorn bowl were inside, right where he'd left them. He picked them up and carried them to the house.

Soon, he would be in bed.

Soon, he would be sleeping.

But his night of scary surprises wasn't over just yet.

In fact, it was just beginning.

13

Before going to bed, this is what Freddie did:

First, he walked straight to the front door and let in Mr. Chewy.

Then he took a bath, put on his pajamas, and brushed his teeth.

He said good-night to his mother, who was watching the news on television.

He said good-night to his father, who was reading a book in his favorite chair.

Then he went to his bedroom. His closet door was open, and he closed it. Then, he climbed into bed. He'd left the flashlight and the scary book on his night stand, and he picked them up.

He turned off the lamp.

And pulled the covers over his head.

He turned on the flashlight, and opened the scary book.

He started reading.

The story was a good one, and Freddie decided that he really, *really* liked this particular book. It was filled with spooky stories about ghosts and goblins and strange creatures.

In fact, he was enjoying the book so much that he almost didn't hear the noise coming from the closet.

Almost.

But he *did* hear it, and he stopped

reading.

He didn't move.

Instead, he listened.

He heard his heart beating.

And his own breathing.

Then he heard the noise again.

A noise in the closet.

He remembered what Darla had told him about super-scary night thingys, and how they can appear at any time, anywhere.

Even in closets.

Slowly . . . very slowly . . . he pulled the covers down beneath his face. Then he pulled the flashlight out.

He aimed the beam across the room at his closet door. There was nothing there.

But the noise came again.

From inside the closet.

And suddenly—

The closet door began to open—all by itself!

14

Freddie screamed.

He screamed so loud that his mother and father bolted from their chairs in the living room and raced to Freddie's bedroom.

The bedroom door burst open.

The light clicked on.

His mom and dad stood in the doorway.

"What's the matter?!?!" Freddie's

mom asked. She was very, very worried.

"Over there!" Freddie pointed frantically. "It's a super-scary night thingy! It's in the closet!"

Freddie's father was very brave, and he walked over to the closet.

He grasped the knob.

And pulled the door open.

There sat Mr. Chewy, next to one of Freddie's tennis shoes. When Freddie had closed the closet door, he hadn't known that Mr. Chewy was inside. The cat had only been trying to get out.

"Is that what you were screaming about?" his father asked. "Mr. Chewy?"

"I . . . I thought that . . . I thought that it was a super-scary night thingy," Freddie stammered.

"Well, I don't know what one of those is," his father said. "But I don't think they're real.   Maybe you shouldn't be reading scary books at night."

After his mother and father left, Mr. Chewy jumped onto the bed.

"Man, you really scared me," Freddie said to the cat as he scratched behind Mr. Chewy's ears.   The cat curled up into a small ball and fell asleep.

And soon, Freddie was asleep, too.

But not for long.

For while Freddie slept, a shadow crept across the floor.

It wasn't his mother's shadow.

It wasn't his father's shadow.

And it certainly wasn't Mr. Chewy's shadow.

The shadow came from something outside.

Something big.

Freddie awoke and saw the shadow of

the creature on his bedroom wall.

    He sat up in bed

    He peered outside the window.

    His jaw fell, and he gasped.

    Freddie Fernortner couldn't believe what he was seeing.

15

An owl!

And not just any owl, either. A great horned owl . . . sitting on a tree branch only a few feet from Freddie's window!

The bird was very large. It was the biggest bird he'd ever seen, except for an eagle he'd seen during a recent bicycle adventure.

He watched the owl for a few minutes. The owl didn't move.

Finally, the owl spread its massive wings. It dipped forward and flew off, disappearing into the darkness.

"Wow," Freddie whispered. *"Mom and Dad aren't going to believe this."*

He wanted to run into their bedroom right now and tell them, but decided not to. If he woke up his parents to tell them he saw a bird outside his window, they might be mad.

He lay back down in bed, still looking out the window. He thought about the owl for a long time, and he remembered an adventure not long ago when he'd turned his bicycle into a fantastic flying machine. He had flown through the sky, too . . . just like a great horned owl.

Soon, Freddie grew tired again, and fell into a deep sleep.

In the morning, he was awakened by

the panicky shouts of his mother. Instantly, he was alarmed.

"*Freddie!*" his mother was shouting. "*Wake up Freddie! Hurry! We've got to get out of the house! There's a super-scary night thingy in here! You were right about them! Super-scary night thingys are real! We've got to get out! Freddie! Freddie!*"

16

"Freddie? Freddie, wake up. Freddie?"

Freddie awoke, struggling in his bed. He was terrified.

"Where is he?!?!" he shouted. He snapped his head around, searching. "Where is he?!?! Where is the super-scary night thingy?!?!"

His mother stood in the doorway with her hands on her hips.

"You were only having a nightmare,

Freddie. It was just a dream."

"You . . . you mean there is no super-scary night thingy in the house?" Freddie asked. Then he looked beneath his bed, just to be sure.

"There is no such thing as a super-scary night thingy," his mother said. "Honestly, Freddie. You're a very smart boy . . . but sometimes your imagination gets out of control. Now . . . rise and shine. Chipper is here. He needs to talk to you, and says it's important. I told him you'd be out in a minute."

"Okay," Freddie said.

His mother left.

What does Chipper want this early in the morning? he wondered. *What could be so important?*

He changed out of his pajamas and put his jeans on. Then he put on a clean Tshirt, then his socks and shoes. He looked in the mirror. His hair was a mess, but it would have to wait.

Chipper was waiting for him in the living room.

"Hi, Freddie," Chipper said.

"Hi, Chipper," Freddie said. "What's going on?"

Chipper's eyes lit up. "Remember last night when we were reading about haunted houses and ghosts?"

"Yeah," Freddie said.

"Well, I told my mom and dad all about it. And do you know what Dad told me?"

Freddie shook his head. "No idea."

"He said that there is a *real* haunted house not far from here! He says it's just a short walk through the woods. Think of it! A *real* haunted house! Wouldn't that be cool to see?"

"Yeah," Freddie agreed, because he really did think it would be cool. He would love to see a real haunted house. Not at night, or anything like that. And he wouldn't want to go inside.

But just to see a real, honest-to-goodness haunted house.

Now *that* would be cool.

"What do you say?" Chipper asked.

"What do you mean?" replied Freddie.

"I mean, do you want to go and find it?"

"Today?" Freddie asked.

Chipper's face was bright. "Yes! It would be so much fun!"

"What about Darla?" Freddie asked.

"I already talked to her. She said that if you wanted to go, she would go. And Mr. Chewy can come, too, of course."

Freddie thought about it. He'd had a lot of scary things happen since last night. Oh, the things that had happened weren't *really* scary. Some of the things were only scary at first . . . like the rabbit in the bushes and the fireflies on the fence. Or Chipper falling into the wading pool.

But if they went to look for the haunted house and actually *found* it . . . well, that might be pretty scary itself.

And that's why Freddie Fernortner thought that it would be cooler than cool.

"Let's do it!" he said to Chipper. "Let's go find the haunted house!"

And that was that. Freddie, Darla, Chipper, and Mr. Chewy were going haunted house hunting.

They would find it, all right.

But they would also find something else:

A ghost.

Soon, all three friends were going to realize that they should never have gone looking for the haunted house . . . .

NEXT:
FREDDIE FERNORTNER, FEARLESS FIRST GRADER

BOOK THREE:

A HAUNTING WE WILL GO

CONTINUE ON TO READ THE FIRST CHAPTER FOR FREE!

1

This is the story of how Freddie Fernortner and his two best friends, Darla and Chipper, along with Freddie's cat Mr. Chewy, discovered a haunted house. It's a very spooky story, too, so you might want to have some lights on while you read it.

One day, Chipper told Freddie and Darla about a haunted house that wasn't far from where they lived.

"My dad told me all about it,"

Chipper explained. "He said that it's only a short walk through the woods."

"Is it really haunted?" Darla asked.

"Yep," Chipper replied, nodding his head. "Dad says that it's been haunted for a long, long time."

"I'll bet it's scary!" Freddie said excitedly.

"That's what my dad said," Chipper piped. "Do you want to see if we can find it?"

Freddie didn't hesitate. "Yeah!" he exclaimed.

"I don't know," Darla said warily. Her eyes grew wide. "There might be ghosts there."

"We won't go inside," Freddie said. "Let's just go and look. I'll bet it's really creepy looking."

Darla thought about it for a minute.

"Well," she said, "I guess it would be okay to just *look* at it."

"It's right over there, through the forest," Chipper pointed. "Dad says it'll only take a few minutes to get there. He says there's even an old trail we can follow."

The three couldn't contain their excitement as they walked across the street, heading toward the deep, dark forest that was behind Chipper's house. Mr. Chewy followed, chewing a wad of gum and blowing bubbles. When the cat was only a small kitten, Freddie taught him how to chew gum and blow bubbles. That's how he got his name.

They walked around the house and found the old trail.

And they followed it.

Deep into the forest.

The thick branches above blocked out the sunlight, and the forest was very dark.

"This is spooky already," Darla said, as she looked around.

And Darla was right.

The forest *was* very spooky.

But things were about to get spookier, as the three first graders were about to find out . . . .

DON'T MISS FREDDIE FERNORTNER, FEARLESS FIRST GRADER

BOOK 3:

A HAUNTING WE WILL GO

ABOUT THE AUTHOR

Johnathan Rand is the author of more than 65 books, with well over 4 million copies in print. Series include **AMERICAN CHILLERS, MICHIGAN CHILLERS, FREDDIE FERNORTNER, FEARLESS FIRST GRADER**, and **THE ADVENTURE CLUB.** He's also co-authored a novel for teens (with Christopher Knight) entitled **PANDEMIA**. When not traveling, Rand lives in northern Michigan with his wife and three dogs. He is also the only author in the world to have a store that sells only his works: **CHILLERMANIA!** is located in Indian River, Michigan. Johnathan Rand is not always at the store, but he has been known to drop by frequently. Find out more at:

www.americanchillers.com

Other books by Johnathan Rand:

Michigan Chillers:

#1: Mayhem on Mackinac Island
#2: Terror Stalks Traverse City
#3: Poltergeists of Petoskey
#4: Aliens Attack Alpena
#5: Gargoyles of Gaylord
#6: Strange Spirits of St. Ignace
#7: Kreepy Klowns of Kalamazoo
#8: Dinosaurs Destroy Detroit
#9: Sinister Spiders of Saginaw
#10: Mackinaw City Mummies
#11: Great Lakes Ghost Ship
#12: AuSable Alligators
#13: Gruesome Ghouls of Grand Rapids
#14: Bionic Bats of Bay City

American Chillers:

#1: The Michigan Mega-Monsters
#2: Ogres of Ohio
#3: Florida Fog Phantoms
#4: New York Ninjas
#5: Terrible Tractors of Texas
#6: Invisible Iguanas of Illinois
#7: Wisconsin Werewolves
#8: Minnesota Mall Mannequins
#9: Iron Insects Invade Indiana
#10: Missouri Madhouse
#11: Poisonous Pythons Paralyze Pennsylvania
#12: Dangerous Dolls of Delaware
#13: Virtual Vampires of Vermont
#14: Creepy Condors of California
#15: Nebraska Nightcrawlers
#16: Alien Androids Assault Arizona
#17: South Carolina Sea Creatures
#18: Washington Wax Museum
#19: North Dakota Night Dragons
#20: Mutant Mammoths of Montana
#21: Terrifying Toys of Tennessee
#22: Nuclear Jellyfish of New Jersey
#23: Wicked Velociraptors of West Virginia
#24: Haunting in New Hampshire
#25: Mississippi Megalodon
#26: Oklahoma Outbreak
#27: Kentucky Komodo Dragons
#28: Curse of the Connecticut Coyotes
#29: Oregon Oceanauts
#30: Vicious Vacuums of Virginia

Freddie Fernortner, Fearless First Grader:

#1: The Fantastic Flying Bicycle
#2: The Super-Scary Night Thingy
#3: A Haunting We Will Go
#4: Freddie's Dog Walking Service
#5: The Big Box Fort
#6: Mr. Chewy's Big Adventure
#7: The Magical Wading Pool
#8: Chipper's Crazy Carnival
#9: Attack of the Dust Bunnies from Outer Space!
#10: The Pond Monster

Adventure Club series:

#1: Ghost in the Graveyard
#2: Ghost in the Grand
#3: The Haunted Schoolhouse

For Teens:

PANDEMIA: A novel of the bird flu and the end of the world
(written with Christopher Knight)

American Chillers Double Thrillers:

Vampire Nation &
Attack of the Monster Venus Melon

Johnathan Rand travels internationally for school visits and book signings! For booking information, call:

1 (231) 238-0338!

www.americanchillers.com

NEW!

WRITTEN AND READ ALOUD BY JOHNATHAN RAND!

available only on compact disc!

Beware! This special audio CD contains six bone-chilling stories written and read aloud by the master of spooky suspense! American Chillers author Johnathan Rand shares six original tales of terror, including *'The People of the Trees'*, *'The Mystery of Coyote Lake'*, *'Midnight Train'*, *'The Phone Call'*, *The House at the End of Gallows Lane'*, and the chilling poem *'Dark Night'*. Turn out the lights, find a comfortable place, and get ready to enter the strange and bizarre world of *CREEPY CAMPFIRE CHILLERS!*

only $9.99!
over 60 minutes of audio!

order online at *www.americanchillers.com*
or call toll-free: 1-888-420-4244!

All AudioCraft books are proudly printed, bound, and manufactured in the United States of America, utilizing American resources, labor, and materials.

USA

WATCH FOR MORE
FREDDIE FERNORTNER,
FEARLESS FIRST GRADER
BOOKS, COMING SOON!